Duck and Hippo
IN THE RAINSTORM

By **JONATHAN LONDON**   Illustrated by **ANDREW JOYNER**

two lions

Published by Two Lions, New York

www.apub.com

Amazon, the Amazon logo, and Two Lions are trademarks of Amazon.com, Inc., or its affiliates.

ISBN-13: 9781503937239
ISBN-10: 1503937232

The illustrations are rendered in brush and ink with wash and pencil and then digitally colored.
Book design by Abby Dening

Printed in China
1 3 5 7 9 10 8 6 4 2

For Sean and Steph, Claire Bear, & sweet Maureen
—J. L.

For William and Charlotte
—A. J.

Duck knocked on Hippo's door.

Knock! Knock! Knock!

"Hi, Duck!" said Hippo.
Duck twirled her umbrella.

"It's spring. *Spring!*"
she said.
"Want to walk in the rain?
It'll be sooo fun!"

"Um . . . ," said Hippo. He was worried about the weather. "*If* you'll share your umbrella." "**Of course!**" said Duck.

So Hippo pulled on his big rubber boots . . .

and went out for a walk in the rain.

But there was no room for Hippo!
He tried walking in front of Duck.
But that didn't work.

He tried walking behind Duck.
But that didn't work.

Then Duck stood on Hippo's feet,
and Hippo held the umbrella.
And that worked just fine!

They puddle-jumped together.

They plopped through
mud together.

And they dropped a stick off a bridge
and watched it rush on down the creek.

SWOOOOOOSH!

Duck said, "Want to sail down the creek?
It'll be like riding a roller coaster!"

"Um . . . ," said Hippo. It looked like
the storm was getting worse.
"*If* you'll share your umbrella."

"Of course!" said Duck.
So Hippo put the umbrella in the creek
and helped his little friend sit down.
But there was no room for Hippo!

Hippo tried sitting in front.
But that didn't work.

Hippo tried sitting in back.
But that didn't work.

Then Duck sat on Hippo's lap,
and that worked just fine!

They swirled around
boulders together.

WHEEEEEEEEE!

They whirled around a crocodile together.

Finally they twirled into a pond
and began to sink!

Hippo totally disappeared!
Duck looked all around for her best friend.

"Hippo! HIPPO! Where *are* you?"

"*Here* I am, silly Duck!" spluttered Hippo,
bursting up for air.

Duck was sitting on Hippo's head!

Hippo sloshed up
out of the pond
and stood dripping on the bank
as the rain crashed down.

"Ahh spring!
Don't you *love* it?"
said Duck. "Want to walk
home in the rain?"

Hippo just stood there,
soaking wet.
"*If* you'll share your umbrella!"
said Hippo.
"Of course!" said Duck.

This time Duck sat on Hippo's shoulders.

She held the umbrella,
and that worked just fine!

But before they could get going,
a terrible wind came ROARING and . . .

WHOOOOO

OOOOOOOOOOOSH!

the umbrella flew up, up, up.
It sailed high over the trees. . . .

And Duck was still hanging on!

"HELLLLLP!" cried Duck.

Hippo raced after Duck
just as fast as his hippo legs would carry him.

Until . . .

Hippo almost tripped over a woodchuck.
But he caught his balance just in time
and kept on running.

And the small but nimble Duck
just missed hitting a tall, tall treetop.

Then down, down, down spun her umbrella,

like a falling leaf . . .

and Duck landed on Hippo's shoulders
right in front of Hippo's house!
"Thanks, Hippo!" cried Duck. "That was *fun!*"
"You're welcome," said Hippo.

"Will you join me for
a warm cup of tea?"
Hippo asked.

"Of course!" said Duck.
She closed her umbrella,

then they both went in the door at the same time.

"WHOOPS!" cried Hippo.
And he **squeeeezed** back out and said,
"After *you*, dear Duck!"

And that worked just fine!